*To the person I need to live: my inner child. She remembers how to imagine and how to express, through writing, who I really am.*

- Marta Arteaga

**Inside My Imagination**


Calle Claveles 10 | Urb Monteclaro | Pozuelo de Alarcón
28223 Madrid | Spain | www.cuentodeluz.com
Original title in Spanish: Dentro de mi imaginación
English translation by Jon Brokenbrow
ISBN: 978-84-15503-59-0
Printed by Shanghai Chenxi Printing Co., Ltd. in PRC, July 2012, print number 1300-01

# Inside My Imagination

by Marta Arteaga

Illustrated by Zuzanna Celej

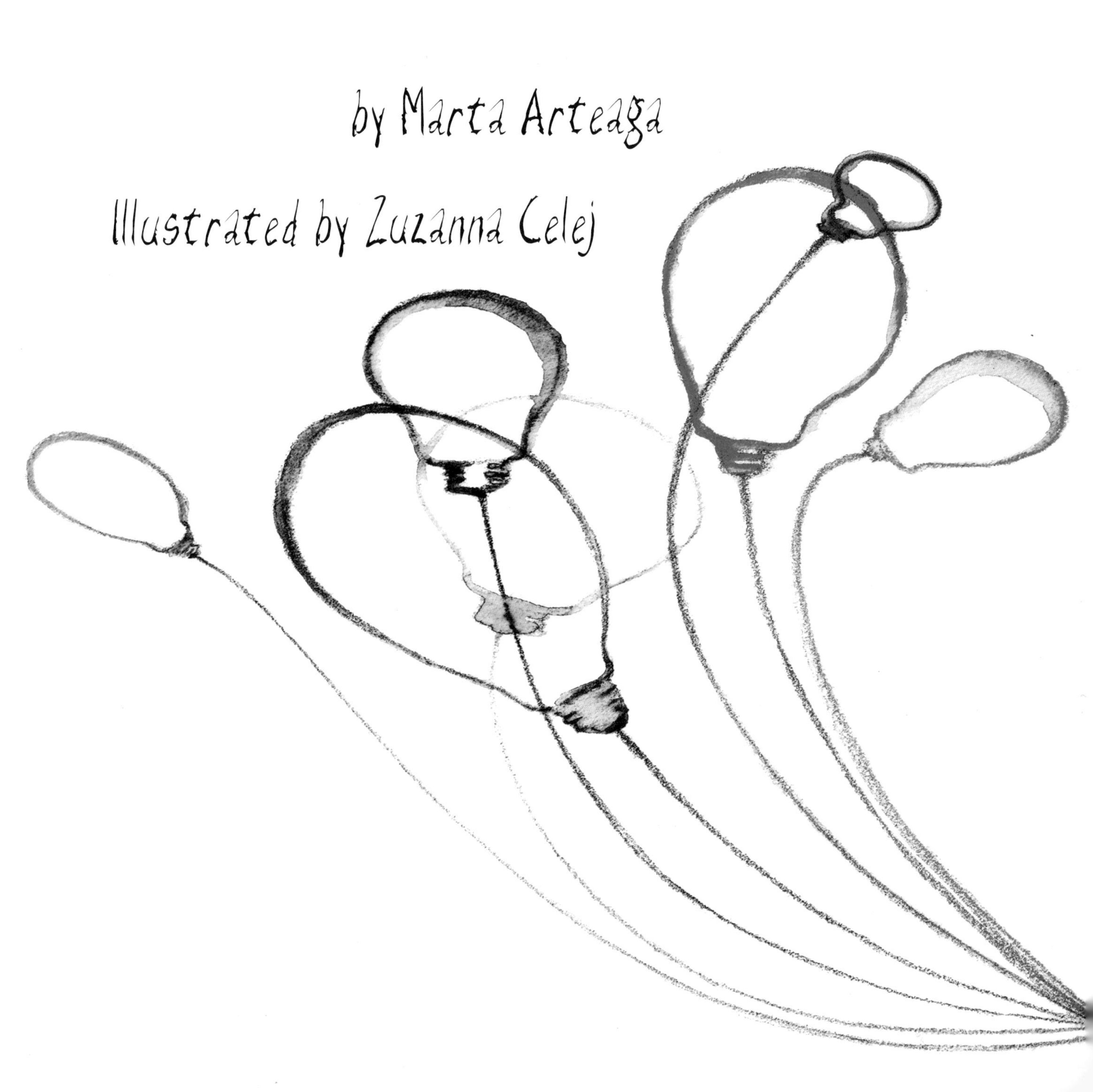

One day I wrote a story just like the ones Mommy reads to me before I go to sleep, a story with lots of lovely words.

One day when I was reading my story, I breathed in one of the words and something magical happened...

I entered my imagination!

It was an amazing paradise!
There were unicorns, fairies, elves and magicians.
They appeared and disappeared whenever I wanted them to.

My imagination is like a sea of thoughts
that float and glide over each other.

Droplets and bubbles contain my ideas that become real
just by looking at them. They swim and swim, trying to
solve the mysteries within me; they appear and disappear,
silently diving far, far away, until there, out on the
horizon, are all of the answers-my answers.

My imagination
is like a land of
clouds of different
shapes.

My imagination is
like a meadow full
of shooting stars.

My imagination is like an enormous music box, where I keep everything I see and hear.

I can keep the sounds of the earth
in a music box-the seas and the rivers,
the crickets, the squirrels leaping through the trees,
and the whisper of the wind in their leaves on those trees...

The day I breathed in my story, I could see my imagination and how it worked inside my mind.

The thinker of my imagination casts her net into the air and catches my ideas.

The more I feed my ideas, the more ideas I have.

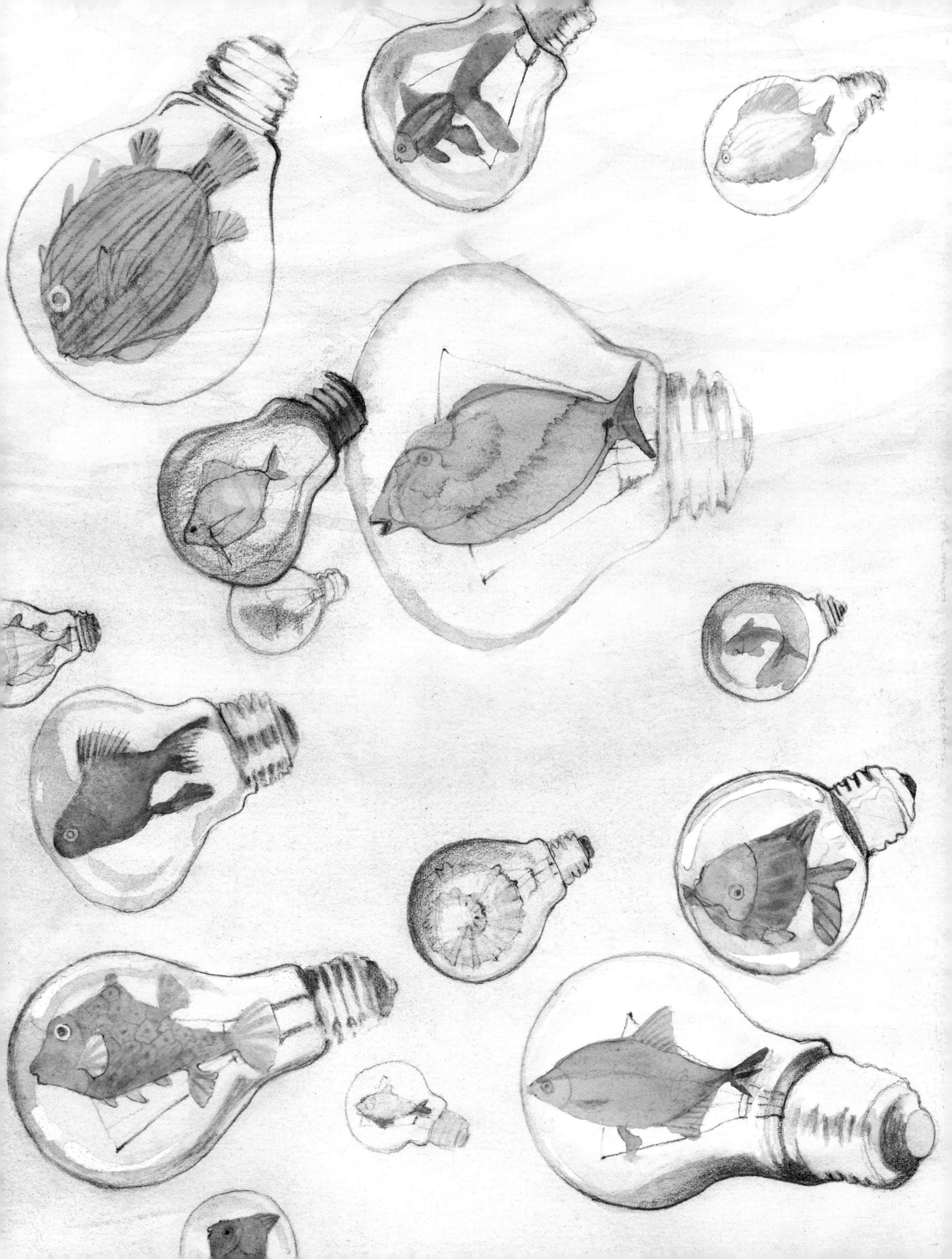

The letters all fit perfectly into place.

abc

Then the words all hold each other's hands...

And they cross the bridge of my imagination that
connects my worlds: the internal and the external.

And they are born, just like I was.